Faith
the Cinderella
Fairy

To Lara, with love

Special thanks to
Rachel Elliot

ORCHARD BOOKS

First published in Great Britain in 2015 by Orchard Books
This edition published in 2016 by The Watts Publishing Group

5 7 9 10 8 6 4

© 2016 Rainbow Magic Limited.
© 2016 HIT Entertainment Limited.
Illustrations © 2015 The Watts Publishing Group Ltd

HIT entertainment

A CIP catalogue record for this book is available from the British Library.

ISBN 978 1 40834 885 7

Printed in Great Britain

MIX
Paper from
responsible sources
FSC® C104740
FSC
www.fsc.org

The paper and board used in this book are made from wood from responsible sources

Orchard Books
An imprint of Hachette Children's Group
Part of The Watts Publishing Group Limited
Carmelite House, 50 Victoria Embankment, London EC4Y 0DZ

An Hachette UK Company
www.hachette.co.uk
www.hachettechildrens.co.uk

Faith
the Cinderella Fairy

by Daisy Meadows

Join the Rainbow Magic Reading Challenge!

Read the story and collect your fairy points to climb the Reading Rainbow online. Turn to the back of the book for details!

This book is worth 5 points.

Jack Frost's Spell

The Fairytale Fairies are in for a shock!
Cinderella won't run at the strike of the clock.
No one can stop me – I've plotted and planned,
And I'll be the fairest Ice Lord in the land.

It will take someone handsome and witty and clever
To stop storybook endings for ever and ever.
But to see fairies suffer great trouble and strife,
Will make me live happily all of my life!

Contents

A Tiptop Morning

"Another gorgeous day at Tiptop Castle!" exclaimed Rachel Walker, throwing open the window and breathing in the crisp morning air.

She was looking out of the tower-top bedroom that she was sharing with her best friend Kirsty Tate. They had been

having a brilliant time at the Fairytale
Festival, and they couldn't wait for this
morning's ballroom-dancing lesson.

"I can't believe how lucky we are,"
said Kirsty, who was brushing her hair at
the beautiful dressing table. "It's amazing
that the festival is being held here, so
close to Tippington – and we've made
some great new friends."

Several children were staying at the castle, and there were fun fairytale activities to enjoy every day. Tippington was Rachel's home town, and Mrs Walker had arranged this special treat for them while Kirsty was staying during half term.

"It was so much fun dressing up yesterday," said Rachel, thinking of their fairy outfits. "I wonder what adventures today will bring!"

"Magical ones, I hope," said Kirsty with a happy smile.

On their first day at the castle, the girls had met their friend Hannah the Happy Ever After Fairy while they were exploring. They had shared many adventures in Fairyland, because they were good friends with the fairies, and they were thrilled when Hannah whisked them off to meet some very special fairies indeed. Julia the Sleeping Beauty Fairy, Eleanor the Snow White Fairy, Faith the Cinderella Fairy and Lacey the Little Mermaid Fairy were the Fairytale Fairies, and they gave the girls *The Fairies' Book of Fairy Tales*. It was a wonderful collection of the girls' four favourite fairy tales, but when they looked inside, the pages were blank.

Thinking about the fairies' shocked faces, Rachel felt a pang of worry.

"It would be wonderful to be able to help another of the Fairytale Fairies," she said.

Kirsty nodded. The fairies had soon discovered that Jack Frost had stolen their magical objects. Without them,

the characters in their fairy tales would
fall out of their stories and get lost! Jack
Frost was planning to rewrite the fairy
tales to star him and his naughty goblins,
and he had taken the fairies' objects to
the human world.

"We should go down to the ballroom,"
said Kirsty, looking at her alarm
clock. "The ballroom-
dancing lesson will be
starting soon and
I don't want
to miss a
second!"

The girls
hurried
down
the spiral
staircase, still

thinking about their fairy friends.
So far, they had helped Julia and
Eleanor to get their magical objects
back. Now Sleeping Beauty and her
prince and Snow White and the seven
dwarves were all back inside their
worlds. But there were still two magical
objects left to find, and many more
fairytale characters to return to their
stories.

The best friends ran all the way
through the castle, but Kirsty
paused when they
reached the ballroom.
Rachel stopped too.

"Are you OK?" she
asked in concern.

"What if I'm not
good enough?" said

Kirsty, sounding suddenly nervous.

"That's why we're having lessons," said Rachel, squeezing her hand. "Anyway, it's only a bit of fun. Don't worry!"

She pushed open the gilt-edged door and stepped inside. The first thing she saw was a young woman standing on a stool, polishing one of the gold-framed mirrors that lined the walls.

"Hello," said Rachel as Kirsty followed her into the room. "Are we in the right place for the dance lesson?"

The young woman turned and gave them a beautiful smile.

"I think so," she said in a longing voice. "The others are over there – it sounds like lots of fun!"

She waved her duster towards the far end of the ballroom, where a small group of children were giggling and

dancing around.

"Thank you very much," said Rachel, wondering why the young woman wasn't joining in with the lesson.

She and Kirsty went to join the others, and then one of the festival organisers entered the room, dressed in a beautiful silver gown.

"Hello, everyone!" she said. "I'm Rosie, your dance instructor for this morning. I hope that this beautiful ballroom will inspire you to dance like true fairytale princes and princesses!"

Two Rude Girls

Looking around, Rachel and Kirsty understood exactly what she meant. The grand ballroom had plush velvet curtains at the windows and a huge crystal chandelier hanging from the ceiling.

"Let's start with a waltz," said Rosie merrily. "I'll give you a demonstration first, and then you try it."

Rosie showed them the whirling waltz steps several times, and then everyone found a partner and started to practise. Rachel and Kirsty danced together. At first they felt as if they were doing quite well, but when they tried to twirl, their feet somehow got tangled up. They ended up in a heap on the floor, giggling helplessly.

"That was awful," said a mean, nasal voice.

"Really dreadful," said another voice, sounding even more spiteful.

Rachel and Kirsty looked up and
saw two girls glaring at them through
narrowed eyes. They
were both wearing
fussy ball gowns
in gaudy colours,
and they looked
as if they had
stuck false
eyelashes on –
very badly.

"What odd
fancy dress," said Kirsty under her
breath.

"What bad manners," said Rachel,
scrambling to her feet. "Come on, let's
try those steps again."

"You shouldn't be allowed on the
dance floor," said one of the girls. "Clear

off right now. We'll show you how
dancing should be done!"

"Let's keep out of their way," said
Rachel in a low voice.

They moved
to the side of
the ballroom
and watched
as the nasty
girls elbowed
their way
past other
dancers
and whirled around, getting all the steps
wrong. Rosie kept stopping them and
trying to show them the correct steps, but
they didn't want to listen. One by one,
the other children in the class came over
to stand with Rachel and Kirsty.

"This isn't much fun," said Emily, who was dancing with Omri. "Let's go and find somewhere else to practise our steps."

Everyone thought this was a very good idea, and they started to slip out of the ballroom. Rachel and Kirsty were last, and as they went to follow the others, something caught Kirsty's eye. She looked up and saw a fairy fluttering down from the crystal chandelier!

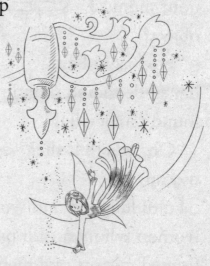

It was Faith the Cinderella Fairy, and she was looking excited.

"Hello, girls!" she said in a happy voice.

"Hello!" said Rachel. "Does your smile mean that you've found your magical object?"

"No," said Faith, her smile fading slightly. "But I have found Cinderella!"

"Oh, where is she?" asked Kirsty with a gasp.

Faith laughed and waved at the young woman who was still polishing the framed mirrors and pictures on the walls.

Rachel and Kirsty could hardly believe it – the young woman was Cinderella!

Cinderella waved back and Faith let out a little sigh.

"I have to find my magical glass slipper soon," she said. "Without it, Cinderella is stuck here in the human world and her fairy tale is ruined."

Just then, the ballroom door opened and Jack Frost swaggered in, walking in a rather lopsided way.

"He's only wearing one shoe," said Rachel in surprise.

"And it's a lady's shoe," Kirsty added.

"It's my shoe," said Faith in a horrified voice. "It's my magical glass slipper, and as long as he's got it, he will be able to do anything he likes with Cinderella's fairy tale."

Rachel glanced over at the bad-tempered girls, but they were too busy arguing about steps with Rosie to notice what was going on at the other end of the ballroom.

"You," Jack Frost snapped, pointing an accusing finger at Cinderella. "Come and clean my Ice Castle from top to bottom right now."

"But I have to find my way home and

finish my cleaning," Cinderella pleaded. "If I don't make the house sparkle, my stepmother won't allow me to go to the ball tonight."

"Tough luck," said Jack Frost. "I'm preparing for a fabulous ball myself tonight, and I'm going to be the star of the show – a dirty kitchen girl isn't going to steal my glory!"

"But it's all I've dreamed about," cried poor Cinderella, clasping her hands together.

"I couldn't care less," Jack Frost barked at her. "You're coming with me!"

With a bolt of icy magic, Jack Frost and Cinderella vanished back to Fairyland.

"Quickly, turn us into fairies!" Kirsty exclaimed. "There's no time to lose!"

Whisked to Fairyland

Faith's wand moved so fast that it was just a blur of magical sparkles. Instantly, the ballroom disappeared and Rachel and Kirsty were in Fairyland before they had time to catch their breath. They found themselves fluttering on gauzy wings, high above Jack Frost's Ice Castle.

It was early evening, and the setting sun shone on the grim, grey battlements.

"That's funny," said Rachel. "There are usually lots of goblins on guard, but I can't see a single one."

"Let's go and find out what's going on," said Faith.

The three fairies swooped down to the battlements and entered the castle through an open door. They flew quickly through damp, dripping corridors, shivering in the sudden darkness. Rachel and Kirsty had been inside the castle

before, so they led the way. When they
were close to the Throne Room, Kirsty
stopped so suddenly that Faith almost
bumped into her.

"Listen!" Kirsty said in a low voice. "I
think I can hear something."

They paused and heard the bad-
tempered squawking voices of several
goblins coming from the room opposite
the Throne Room.

"What a racket!" said Faith. "Come
on, let's find out what they're shouting
about."

The door was ajar, so it was easy for
the three tiny fairies to slip inside without
being noticed. They flew up to a high
curtain rail, tucked themselves out of
sight and gazed down upon a wintry
ballroom.

Icicle chandeliers hung from the centre of the ceiling, and stalactites were clustered around it, flashing blue and white. There were several goblins on their hands and knees, polishing the wooden floor. Others were painting snowflakes on the tall windows and twining blue lights into some ragged-

looking potted plants. Rachel spotted
goblins dressed as chefs, each carrying
a platter piled high with green and blue
cupcakes. Three goblins were squashed
around a small desk, writing invitations
very slowly and elbowing each other
as they wrote. So far they had only
completed the first line:

> You are hereby invited to a spectacular ball
> in honour of a mystery guest.

"Look," Kirsty whispered, nudging Rachel and Faith. "There's Cinderella."

Still wearing her ragged clothes, Cinderella was busily dusting a huge silver throne at the front of the ballroom.

"Poor thing," said Rachel. "How can we help her escape?"

"First we have to find Jack Frost and get my magical glass slipper back," said Faith. "Then Cinderella will be able to return to her story."

Just then, Kirsty noticed a trail of richly

embroidered clothes scattered across a grand staircase behind the throne.

"I bet Jack Frost made that mess," she said. "He would expect Cinderella or the goblins to tidy up for him."

"Let's investigate!" said Rachel, feeling excited.

Keeping hidden from the goblins, they flew over to the clothes and fluttered up the staircase. Kirsty saw that Cinderella looked very unhappy and wished they could comfort her, but she knew that they mustn't risk being seen.

At the top of the stairs, the trail of beautiful clothes led them to a very big walk-in dressing room. The door was wide open, and a steady line of goblins was walking in with armfuls of puffy, lacy, exuberant outfits.

"No, no, NO!" Jack Frost screeched from inside the room. "Imbeciles! My outfit has to be the best. These are all disgusting – take them away!"

A goblin came flying out of the room and landed on his bottom. A mound of pastel-coloured fabric followed him and fell on his head. While the other goblins were sniggering, the fairies slipped into the dressing room and hid behind a curtain. They found themselves next to a tall window, which looked down over the snow-covered forest beside the castle. Faith peeped through the curtain, and Rachel and Kirsty peered over her shoulders.

In the centre of the room, Jack Frost was standing in front of an enormous three-way mirror, frowning at his

reflection. He was wearing green robes and a goblin was sitting at his feet with a mouthful of pins.

"What about this one, Your Iciness?" asked another goblin.

"I've told you, you have to call me Cinderfrost!" Jack Frost yelled. "And you had better find me the perfect ball outfit – or else!"

A Moaning
Mystery Guest

Jack Frost tore the robes off and kicked
them away, holding out his hand for
the next outfit. This was pale blue with
white frills. He pulled it on with rough
hands, and a goblin tied a yellow sash
around his waist.

"That doesn't match!" Jack Frost howled. "Take it off! Hurry up – you're too slow!"

"He's still wearing my magical glass slipper," Faith said, noticing as Jack aimed a kick at a goblin who had tied the wrong-coloured sash.

"How can we get it off his foot?" Kirsty wondered aloud.

Rachel was looking out of the window, and noticed two goblins running away from the castle through the snow, each carrying a large postbag.

"They must be going to deliver the invitations," she murmured.

"This isn't good enough for Cinderfrost!" Jack Frost snarled, drawing Rachel's attention back to the dressing room.

"What about a diamond-encrusted pendant?" suggested a goblin in a wheedling voice.

"I know!" Rachel whispered. "We need a pair of shoes that Jack Frost will like better than the magical glass slipper!"

Faith waved her wand at the enormous wardrobe and a pair of sparkly ice-blue shoes appeared. A goblin seized them at once.

"Look, these are blue like the beautiful robes," he squeaked. "They're just the thing!"

The goblins gathered round in admiration as Jack put one of the sparkly shoes on.

"A perfect fit!" said one.

"Divine!" said another. "Put on the other one!"

The fairies leaned forward, keeping their fingers crossed. But Jack Frost shook his head.

"I'm not taking this glass slipper off," he snapped.

The goblin at his feet spat the pins out of his mouth.

"But it's too big," he said. "The sparkly ones look much better."

"I'll just wear one of each," Jack Frost declared.

The goblins started to snigger, and Jack Frost glowered at them.

"You're no help at all!" he shouted. "I need a fairy godmother to help me dress for the ball."

He stamped the foot that was wearing the magical glass slipper, and there was a sudden puff of glittering fairy dust. When it cleared, a kind-looking elderly fairy was fluttering in the air beside Jack Frost. Her wings shimmered with all the colours of the rainbow, and her snow-white hair was swept up into an elegant bun.

"Good evening, Cinderfrost," she said in a low voice. "Why have you called for me?"

"Give me the perfect party outfit now," said Jack Frost. "And you had better make it more beautiful than any other outfit that's ever been. Cinderfrost is going to be the most spectacular sight ever, and I want everyone else to look awful next to me!"

Rachel and Kirsty wondered if the Fairy Godmother would refuse such a rude demand, but she simply sighed and waved her wand. Suddenly Jack was wearing an ice-blue flowing cloak that glittered with thousands of tiny sequins. Long, floaty sleeves covered his arms and shoulders, and a diamond crown sparkled in his spiky hair.

Jack Frost gasped and gazed at his reflection, turning this way and that to see every inch of the beautiful outfit.

"It's my favourite colour," he said at last. "This is the perfect outfit for Cinderfrost!"

The goblins around him heaved sighs of relief and several of them collapsed into a heap of clothes.

"It's about time," said one, glancing up at a clock on the wall. "You've taken ages to choose."

"I'm going to make a grander entrance than any royal has ever dreamed of making," Jack Frost boasted. "Everyone will be looking at me! My carriage is waiting at the back door, and then I'll ride to the front to make my entrance. They'll all be waiting in the ballroom for the most dazzling mystery guest that ever was – Cinderfrost!"

"I've got an idea," said Rachel, sounding suddenly excited. "Faith, can you disguise us as Cinderella's stepsisters?"

Faith looked uncertain.

"It would take some very special magic," she said. "I can do it, but I'll need the Fairy Godmother to help me."

Kirsty peeped into the room again. Jack was staring at his reflection, entranced. The goblins were cackling as they rolled around among the unwanted outfits. No one was looking at the Fairy Godmother.

"Psst!" said Kirsty. "Fairy Godmother!"

The Fairy Godmother turned and her face crinkled into a smile when she saw Kirsty. She fluttered behind the curtain to join them.

"Well, I didn't expect to meet little fairies here," she said. "What can I do for you?"

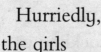

Hurriedly, the girls whispered their plan to her. She agreed at once, and together, she and Faith waved their wands. Rachel and Kirsty stared at each other as their eyes grew narrower, their noses more pointy and their mouths mean and tight-lipped. A few seconds later they were towering over the fairies, and they were wearing

gaudy ball gowns
in ugly colours.

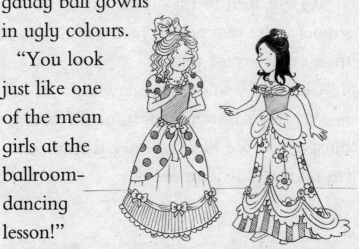

"You look
just like one
of the mean
girls at the
ballroom-
dancing
lesson!"
Kirsty said at once.

"You too," Rachel replied. "Oh Kirsty,
they must have been Cinderella's real
stepsisters. I had no idea!"

There was no time to talk about it
now. The girls pushed the curtain aside
and walked up behind Jack Frost, trying
to feel brave. Remembering how the
stepsisters had spoken, Rachel put on the
meanest voice she could manage.

"It's our turn to try on the glass
slipper," she snapped at Jack Frost. "It's
much too big for you."

"Clear off," said Jack, scowling.

"But that's how our story goes," Kirsty
burst out. "We have to have a chance to
try on the glass slipper."

"I'm not bothered how your story goes!" Jack Frost yelled at her. "I'm Cinderfrost and this is my story now, so no one is going to try on my glass slipper! Go away!"

Twilight in Fairyland

Badly disappointed that their plan hadn't worked, Rachel and Kirsty ducked back behind the curtain. Faith waved her wand and turned them back into fairies. Then she gave them a big hug.

"Thank you for trying," she said. "Jack Frost is too stubborn for words."

"We'll just have to try something else," said Rachel in a determined voice.

The Fairy Godmother gave them a gentle smile.

"I wish I could stay to help you, but someone else is calling for my help," she said. "I hope that you can stop Jack Frost from spoiling my poor Cinderella's story. She's such a sweet girl."

She held up her wand and twirled into the air, then disappeared in a silvery twinkle. For a moment, Kirsty thought that she heard the sound of far-off bells. Even though she was worried about Faith's magical glass slipper, she couldn't help a little quiver of excitement. She had never met a fairy godmother before.

The space in the window alcove had grown darker – it was twilight in

Fairyland. Rachel and Kirsty peered out of the window and were surprised to see lots of fairies fluttering down from the starlit sky. They were all wearing beautiful ball gowns, and their jewelled necklaces, tiaras and bracelets were glistening in the half light.

"I expect they've all been invited to the ball," said Rachel. "Goodness me, Jack must be planning a very grand evening indeed – he doesn't normally like fairies anywhere near his castle."

"I suppose he needed lots of guests, just like in the Cinderella fairy tale," said Kirsty. "Oh, of course!"

Rachel and Faith looked at her with hope in their eyes. Did she have an idea to get back the magical glass slipper?

"We should have thought about the fairy tale from the start," said Kirsty. "Do you remember how Cinderella's dress turns back to rags on the stroke of midnight?"

"Yes, and her glass slipper comes off as she runs out of the ballroom," Rachel added.

"Midnight is a very important time in this story," Kirsty went on. "Perhaps we need to see what Cinderfrost will do when the clock strikes twelve. If the glass slipper is loose, it might come off if he has to hurry."

Faith smiled – she understood exactly what Kirsty had in mind! With a wave of her wand she changed the clock on the wall so it said five minutes to twelve. She also made the glass slipper grow just a little larger. Almost at once, one of the goblins glanced up at the clock and gave a loud gasp of surprise.

"Cinderfrost, look at the time!" he squawked. "You're going to miss the ball!"

Jack Frost let out a cry of dismay.

"Get out of my way!" he bellowed. "I've got to make my grand entrance!"

He ran out of the room in a panic, still wearing Faith's too-big magical glass slipper on one foot and the ice-blue shoe on the other. The fairies followed him at top speed as he pelted down the back stairs.

"Oh, please let his glass slipper fall off!" said Rachel under her breath.

Jack stumbled as he reached the last step, but his glass slipper stayed on. He dashed out through the back door to where an ornate silver carriage was waiting, with a goblin footman standing at the back in a green-and-gold uniform.

"Hurry up!" the footman shouted when he saw Jack Frost. "I've been out here for ages and it's freezing."

"Shut up, frog-face," yelled Jack Frost.

He took a flying leap into the carriage, landing in a heap of ice-blue frills. His heel half-popped out of the magical glass slipper and the fairies darted forwards, but the door slammed shut in their faces and the carriage set off. They stared at each other in dismay.

"Let's fly ahead and hide at the entrance," said Kirsty. "I've got an idea!"

Cinderella at the Ball

While Kirsty explained her plan, they zoomed around the side of the castle towards the main entrance. There were two large statues of Jack Frost on either side of the castle door, and Rachel and Kirsty hid behind one, while Faith tucked herself behind the other. They were ready.

The carriage rumbled to a halt
between the statues, and a goblin butler
opened the castle door. The fairies could
see that the entrance hall was lined with
curious fairies.

Everyone stared
as Jack Frost
stepped
out of his
carriage
and
adjusted
his tiara.

"The
mystery
guest has
arrived!"

announced the
goblin butler in an important voice.

Smirking, Jack Frost stepped forward to greet his admirers. But as he drew level with the statues…

"Now!" shouted Kirsty.

She, Rachel and Faith leaped out from their hiding place and Jack Frost jumped high into the air in surprise.

At last the magical glass slipper fell from his foot and Rachel dived down to grab it. Before Jack Frost could understand what was happening, the magical glass slipper was back in Faith's hands at last.

In a flurry of golden sparkles,
Cinderella appeared in the castle
doorway dressed in a glimmering ball
gown. Her tiara sparkled in the starlight,
and all the fairies cheered as she waved
to them. Rachel and Kirsty cheered
too, and Cinderella saw them and gave
a happy smile. Then, as everyone was

gasping at her beauty, she shimmered and faded out of sight.

"Where has she gone?" cried a disappointed fairy nearby.

"She's gone back to her fairy tale, where she belongs," said Faith, before turning to the girls with a warm smile. "And now it's time for you two to go back where you belong. Thank you for everything you've done to help me and the other Fairytale Fairies so far.

Without you, the world would be a far less magical place."

"We've loved helping – and meeting some of our favourite characters in real life," said Rachel.

"It's an honour," Kirsty added.

As Jack Frost stamped his feet and gnashed his teeth, Faith, Rachel and Kirsty shared a big hug. Then Faith waved her wand and the girls blinked, their eyes filled with fairy dust. Seconds later, they were once again standing in the ballroom at Tiptop Castle. Rosie, the dance instructor, was waltzing around the room with Omri.

"Cinderella's bossy stepsisters have disappeared," said Kirsty, feeling relieved.

"Yes, and all the other children are back," Rachel added, looking at the crowd of their new friends. "Come on, let's go and join in!"

They shared a wonderful lesson with their friends, with plenty of giggles along the way. By the end of it, everyone was able to waltz around the ballroom, twirling and spinning without falling over.

"Excellent!" Rosie called, clapping her hands together. "You've all picked up the steps really well. That's the end of the lesson, but I have a surprise for you. Tomorrow night, you will be using your new dancing skills at a fairytale ball – right here in Tiptop Castle!"

There were gasps and thrilled squeals from everyone, and they all started chattering at once.

"What shall we wear?"

"What time does it start?"

"I can't wait!"

Rachel and Kirsty threw their arms around each other and jumped up and down.

"Today's just getting better and better!" said Rachel with a laugh.

The fairytale ball was the only thing anyone could talk about for the rest of the day. That evening, the girls went to bed with a lovely, tingly feeling of hope and delight.

"It's almost as exciting as Christmas Eve," said Kirsty as she snuggled under the covers. "I wonder what the ball will be like."

"Let's read the story of Cinderella," said Rachel, grabbing *The Fairies' Book of Fairy Tales* and hopping into bed beside her best friend.

Side by side, they turned the pages until they reached Cinderella's wonderful story. All the characters were just where they belonged, together with Sleeping

Beauty and Snow White. It was good to see the words and pictures back in the book as if they had never been away. They took turns to read a page at a time.

"... and they lived happily ever after," finished Kirsty, turning the last page of the story.

Their happy smiles faded slightly when they saw that the following pages were blank. The story of *The Little Mermaid* was still missing, and the girls knew that Lacey must be longing to find her magical object.

"I hope that we can help Lacey to find her magical object before the fairytale ball tomorrow," said Rachel, putting *The Fairies' Book of Fairy Tales* on Kirsty's bedside table and climbing into her own four-poster bed.

Kirsty nodded and gave a sleepy yawn.

"It's been an exciting day, hasn't it?" she said. "I'm so glad we were able to help Faith and Cinderella."

"Me too," said Rachel. "I wonder what adventures tomorrow will bring!"

Meet the
Fairytale Fairies

Kirsty and Rachel are going to a Fairytale Festival!
Can they help get the Fairytale Fairies' magical objects
back from Jack Frost, before he ruins all the stories?

www.rainbowmagicbooks.co.uk

**Now it's time for Kirsty and
Rachel to help…**

Lacey the Little Mermaid Fairy

Read on for a sneak peek…

"I'm sure it's this way," said Rachel
Walker, pointing to a twisty stone
staircase. She lifted a rolled-up banner
onto her shoulder and began to tiptoe
down the steps.

Kirsty Tate followed behind her best
friend. In her arms she was carrying a
large cardboard box.

"This must be the east turret," she
decided, stopping to peek out of an
arched window. Rachel paused to look,
too. From where they were standing the
girls had a perfect view of the courtyard
of Tiptop Castle. Kirsty beamed – it was

like a scene from a fairy tale! A fountain carved in the shape of a shell bubbled merrily in the middle of the cobbles and sweet-smelling pink roses curled up the columns around the sides. She wouldn't have been surprised to glimpse a royal princess wandering along the walkways or a knight ride in on a glossy white stallion.

"What a magical place," declared Rachel, "We're so lucky to be staying here!"

"I wouldn't have missed it for anything," agreed Kirsty, following her friend through an oak archway at the bottom of the stairs.

Rachel and Kirsty had been sharing an amazing spring holiday at Tiptop Castle. Being together was always a dream come true, but this week had been extra-special. The friends had taken part in the castle's annual Fairytale Festival. They'd spent their days dressing up in beautiful costumes, acting out stories and drawing pictures of all their favourite characters. Every night when the fun and games were over, the girls got to sleep in a real castle bedchamber! It was a world away from their homes in Tippington and Wetherbury – it was a place full of tapestries, glittering chandeliers and four-poster beds.

Read **Lacey the Little Mermaid Fairy** to find out what adventures are in store for Kirsty and Rachel!

Calling all parents, carers and teachers!
The Rainbow Magic fairies are here to help
your child enter the magical world of reading.
Whatever reading stage they are at, there's
a Rainbow Magic book for everyone!
Here is Lydia the Reading Fairy's guide to
supporting your child's journey at all levels.

Starting Out

Our Rainbow Magic Beginner Readers are perfect for first-time readers who are just beginning to develop reading skills and confidence. Approved by teachers, they contain a full range of educational levelling, as well as lively full-colour illustrations.

Developing Readers

Rainbow Magic Early Readers contain longer stories and wider vocabulary for building stamina and growing confidence. These are adaptations of our most popular Rainbow Magic stories, specially developed for younger readers in conjunction with an Early Years reading consultant, with full-colour illustrations.

Going Solo

The Rainbow Magic chapter books – a mixture of series and one-off specials – contain accessible writing to encourage your child to venture into reading independently. These highly collectible and much-loved magical stories inspire a love of reading to last a lifetime.

www.rainbowmagicbooks.co.uk

"Rainbow Magic got my daughter reading chapter books. Great sparkly covers, cute fairies and traditional stories full of magic that she found impossible to put down" – Mother of Edie (6 years)

"Florence LOVES the Rainbow Magic books. She really enjoys reading now" Mother of Florence (6 years)

Read along the Reading Rainbow!

Well done – you have completed the book!

This book was worth 1 star.

See how far you have climbed on the Reading Rainbow.
The more books you read, the more stars you can colour in
and the closer you will be to becoming a Royal Fairy!

Do you want to print your own Reading Rainbow?

1) Go to the Rainbow Magic website

2) Download and print out the poster

3) Colour in a star for every book you finish
and climb the Reading Rainbow

4) For every step up the rainbow,
you can download your very own certificate

There's all this and lots more at
rainbowmagicbooks.co.uk

You'll find activities, stories, a special newsletter
AND you can search for the fairy with your name!